MORTAL KOMBAT

"Welcome!" Shang Tsung said. "You are here to compete in Mortal Kombat, the greatest of all tournaments. You should be proud! Each of you has been chosen for your excellence, your skill, and your courage! You are the best fighters of your generation, worthy to represent the Realm of Earth, and the Realm of Outworld!

"You all are witnesses to a great turning point in the history of the world. Treasure these moments as if they were your last...!"

With a dozen color photos from the hit movie!

MORTAL KOMBAT

MARTIN DELRIO

TOR

A TOM DOHERTY ASSOCIATES BOOK
NEW YORK

This is a work of fiction. All the characters and events portrayed in this book are fictitious, and any resemblance to real people or events is purely coincidental.

MORTAL KOMBAT

Copyright © 1995 by New Line Productions, Inc. All Rights Reserved.

Mortal Kombat® and the Mortal Kombat dragon logo are trademarks of Midway® Manufacturing Company. Used under license.

Cover art by R.E. Aaron Copyright © 1995 by New Line Productions, Inc.

A Tor book
Published by Tom Doherty Associates, Inc.
175 Fifth Avenue
New York, NY 10010

Tor® is a registered trademark of Tom Doherty Associates, Inc.

ISBN: 0-812-54453-6

First edition: August 1995

Printed in the United States of America

0 9 8 7 6 5 4 3 2 1

ONE

❖

JOHNNY CAGE, the movie star, stood on the set of his latest film. He was looking at a scroll. The scroll was small, twisted around a stick of black wood. It was decorated with a logo showing a dragon's head in a circle.

"This is the most ancient tournament in the world," said the man who had brought the scroll. "It's held on an island in the South China Sea. All of the participants are sworn to secrecy. The best fighters in the world are invited. If you win the tournament, you'll win their respect."

"How do I get there?" Johnny asked.

"There will be a ship at Pier Forty in Hong Kong, tomorrow night. Be on it."

Half the world away, in Hong Kong, the smoke was thick in the Techno Club.

"Are you sure she'll follow me down here?" Kano asked. The crime boss stood in his office, watching as Sonya Blade, an American Special Forces officer, made her way across the dance floor toward him, a pistol in her hand.

"You killed her partner," the sorcerer Shang Tsung replied. "She'll follow you anywhere. Just make sure she gets on that ship."

Kano turned and climbed down a ladder into a trapdoor set in the floor. Minutes later, when Sonya burst into the office, she followed him.

Liu Kang and his grandfather stood in front of the Temple of Rayden. Liu's brother, Chan, had died there scarcely a day before.

"What happened?" Liu asked.

"After you left for America, he followed in your footsteps, preparing for the tournament," Grandfather replied.

"The tournament," Liu said. "Wasn't it enough that you filled my head with that nonsense?"

"To save the world is not nonsense," Grandfather

said. "We all believe in it, including your brother. He trained very hard. But he could never be as good as you."

"Grandfather," Liu said, "I dreamed Chan's death. And in my dream I saw his killer."

"You saw the demon sorcerer Shang Tsung," Grandfather replied.

Liu Kang and Grandfather went inside the Temple. Liu said to the chief priest, "I want to represent the Order of Light at the tournament."

"For what reason?" the chief priest asked.

"The man who killed my brother will be there," Liu replied.

"That cannot be the only reason for going," the chief priest said, "or you will fail."

"Oh yes, I forgot," Liu said. "We're fighting for the fate of the world."

An old beggar entered the door of the temple. "Why do you want to fight?" he asked.

"Shang Tsung, the man who killed my brother, will be at that tournament," Liu replied. "It's my responsibility."

"That is why you left the temple and ran away, isn't it?" the beggar asked. "The great tournament was too much responsibility. Vengeance is so much simpler. You didn't even believe in the tournament yesterday. So now you're going to win?"

"Yes, I am," Liu replied. "Who are you?"

"I am Rayden, the god of lightning. In the Great Tournament five centuries ago, your ancestor Kung Lao defeated Shang Tsung the sorcerer," Rayden said. "You are Kung Lao's last living descendant. But you reject all you've learned. You don't believe in the teachings and you don't believe in yourself."

"If you are Rayden, why did you let Chan die?" Liu asked.

"The gods do not control men's destiny," Rayden said.

"I've had enough of this," Liu said. "I'm going to find my brother's killer at the tournament, with or without your consent!"

Liu stormed away from the temple.

"He isn't ready, my lord," Grandfather said.

"I know," Rayden replied. "But there is no one else. You shouldn't have tried to replace him with his brother. Whether any of you like it or not, Liu Kang is the chosen one."

That night, a ghostly ship pulled into Hong Kong Harbor. Its sails were tattered and its planks were warped. Barnacles stuck to its sides. Seaweed was piled up on the deck.

Sonya saw Kano get aboard. She moved to

follow him.

She ran into Johnny Cage.

"Hey, you!" Johnny shouted.

"Out of my way," Sonya said, and boarded the ship.

Sonya went belowdecks looking for Kano, but was unable to find him. By the time she got back on deck, the ship was under way, creaking in the wind. There she met Liu, Johnny, and Rayden.

"Listen!" Rayden said. "The time for doubt is past. The time for your petty quarrels is past. You have embarked on a sacred mission. You have been chosen to defend the Realm of Earth in a tournament called Mortal Kombat!"

"Defend it from whom?" Sonya asked.

"Your world is but one of many parallel realms," Rayden said. "One of them is a forsaken land called Outworld, ruled by an immortal who has crowned himself emperor. Now he seeks new worlds to conquer and enslave."

"If he's so powerful," Johnny asked, "why doesn't he just invade us?"

"To enter the Realm of Earth, the emperor's demon sorcerer, Shang Tsung, and his warriors must win ten straight victories in Mortal Kombat against ten generations of Earth's best fighters. They have won nine. This will be the tenth tournament."

"A handful of people on a leaky boat are going to save the world?" Sonya asked.

"There is one in Outworld whom you may trust," Rayden said. "The Princess Kitana. She is the emperor's ward, and his most dangerous adversary. Shang will do anything to keep you from speaking with her—especially you, Liu Kang."

The sky began to burn with multicolored lights. Weird ghostly shapes chased each other across the sky. The wind began to howl. Shang Tsung the sorcerer looked on in satisfaction.

"It has begun!" Shang said.

TWO

✦✦✦

THE SHIP lay at anchor near a beach at a deserted island. The island rose high above the sea, a tall spike of rock. The rock rose until it was enveloped in clouds, then rose higher still, a mile into the air. Only a narrow stairway joined the beach to the top of the island. Sonya, Liu, and Johnny, along with hundreds of other fighters, got out of the ship and began to climb.

The stairway was long and steep. At the top of the stairs was a pleasant garden, filled with blooming flowers and green grass. Amid the grass and flowers stood statues of the great champions of Mortal Kombats in the past.

A woman stood among the statues. She was dressed in red silk and surrounded by ladies in waiting. She looked at Liu as he and his companions walked past.

"When a woman looks at you like that it means something," Johnny said.

"It means she's a bimbo," Sonya commented.

Johnny, Liu, and Sonya walked on in the direction of the Great Hall, a huge building with a golden roof built into the side of a mountain. No sooner had they gone out of sight than Shang Tsung appeared from behind a statue of an alien, lizard-like fighter.

The demon sorcerer spoke, although who he was speaking to wasn't apparent.

"Princess Kitana," Shang said. He was looking in the direction of the woman in red silk. "She is the emperor's ward. I don't trust her, she is our most dangerous adversary. Watch her, Reptile. She must not make contact with the others. Especially Liu Kang."

Shang Tsung walked in the direction of the hall. A moment later, the statue under which he had stood seemed to come to life. It was the reptilian fighter, to whom Shang Tsung had spoken, so cleverly camouflaged that he seemed to be made of stone. Reptile slithered down the pedestal and ran away in the direction of the princess.

That night there was a feast in the Great Hall on the island. Drums beat fiercely.

"Welcome!" Shang said. "You are here to compete in Mortal Kombat, the greatest of all tournaments. You should be proud! Each one of you has been chosen for your excellence, your skill, and your courage! You are the best fighters of your generation, worthy to represent the Realm of Earth, and the Realm of Outworld!

"Tomorrow morning," Shang continued, "the great tournament begins. Your opponents will be chosen by lot. The winner of each combat will progress to the next, until only one remains! Some will even have the privilege of fighting Prince Goro, the reigning champion. You are all witnesses to a great turning point in the history of the world. Treasure these moments as if they were your last. And now, a taste of things to come!"

A strange creature stalked into the hall. It was dressed in strange bionic armor which covered its entire body, while a helmet of bone covered its face and head. The Outworld warrior whirled a long spear through the air with a swishing sound. When it came to the center of the Great Hall, it gave a loud cry of defiance.

Down from the dais came a ninja dressed in black and blue. This was Sub-Zero, one of Shang Tsung's servants.

The creature and the ninja faced one another in the center of the hall. The creature shook its lance and prepared to strike. The ninja merely stood in a defensive stance, but a faint blue light began to glow around his hands.

All at once, the creature charged Sub-Zero. The creature jumped at the ninja. Sub-Zero raised one of his hands. A blast of pure cold shot out, striking the creature in mid-air. Then the ninja stepped aside. The creature hit the floor and shattered. It broke into a thousand tiny, frozen pieces.

The demon sorcerer stood watching in silence from the high table.

"Flawless victory," Shang said.

From his seat in the Great Hall, Johnny sat and stared. The creature had smashed to pieces right next to him.

" 'Come to a little tournament,' the man says," Johnny muttered. " 'Be good for the career,' he says ..."

Shang Tsung stood and walked from the hall. Two ninjas walked behind him. As soon as Shang had passed by them, Liu stood and began to follow the evil magician.

"Where are you heading?" Johnny asked. He caught Liu's arm to stop him from going anywhere.

"I'm going after Shang Tsung," Liu said in a reasonable tone of voice.

"You can't," Johnny said. "Remember what Rayden told you?"

"Rayden didn't say anything to me," Sonya said. She also stood and turned in the direction the sorcerer had gone.

"Shang Tsung knows where Kano's hiding," the young woman said, and strode out of the hall.

Johnny watched her go.

"You gotta admire her," he said. "When she sets her mind on something ..."

"It's not her mind you're admiring," Liu interrupted with a smile.

"I'm going to follow her," Johnny said. "She might need help."

Johnny started after Sonya. Liu shrugged, then hurried to catch up with the actor. Liu and Johnny left the Great Hall together.

Shang Tsung walked through the garden full of statues. This time he took a different path, one which led him to a high cliff. In the base of the cliff there was a tunnel leading into the black depths of the realm of Shokan. Torches burned on either side of the tunnel opening. Shang and his two ninjas entered the tunnel, not looking back.

Sonya was hiding near the tunnel mouth, using all of her Army skills to follow Shang Tsung without being seen. She spotted Johnny and Liu, and stopped them from entering the tunnel after Shang and the ninjas.

"What are you doing here?" Sonya asked.

"We're helping you," Johnny said.

"How many times do I have to tell you?" Sonya hissed. "I don't need your help. I can take care of myself."

"We can't help it. It's a guy thing," Johnny replied.

"What are you doing?" Sonya asked, turning to Liu.

"I'm following him," Liu replied. He pointed in the direction Shang had gone.

"I work alone," Sonya said.

"Shang Tsung is mine," Liu said. Without another word he entered the tunnel and vanished in the dark.

Sonya followed Liu in. A moment later, Johnny picked up one of the torches which burned beside the tunnel's entrance and followed the other two.

The inside of the tunnel opened out into a wide cavern. The floor was a maze of pathways between deep cracks. The torch Johnny was carrying provided the only light for the three companions.

Suddenly, the torch began to flicker.

"How can you possibly know where you're going?" Sonya asked Johnny. "You can't even keep the torch lit."

"What do you mean?" Johnny replied. "The torch is fine."

"That torch is going to go out," Sonya told him. The torch gave another flicker. It was burning with a low, blue flame.

"It is not going to go out," Johnny said confidently.

"Do you want me to carry the torch?" Sonya asked.

"No, I don't want you to carry the torch."

"Let me carry it."

"The torch is fine."

"Give it to me." Sonya tried to grab the torch. Instead she knocked it out of Johnny's hand. The torch fell into one of the crevices between the pathways. It fell for a long time. Its light grew dim, then went out. A long time after that came the sound of the torch hitting bottom.

"Face it, we're lost," Sonya said.

"When you get to know me better," Johnny said, "you'll realize that I never get lost. I never have to ask for directions, and I always find a parking spot. Usually there's money in the meter."

"Look!" Liu said. "There's a light down there. Listen."

The three could hear a low sound, like men's voices, but they couldn't make out the words. A patch of light, like reflected firelight, glowed in the darkness ahead of them. And in the patch of light Johnny could see a shadow. It looked like a man's shadow—but the shadow had four arms.

"I don't suppose there's a little guy down there, doing shadow puppets," Johnny whispered.

"I don't think so," Sonya whispered back.

"Come on," Liu said. He led the way toward the light.

Soon they came to a cavern full of stalactites and stalagmites. It was lit by blazing torches. Black jaguars roamed about the cavern. A narrow ledge ran around the room. Johnny, Liu, and Sonya followed the ledge to a place where they could see who was in the cavern room.

Two people sat at a table heaped high with food. One of them was Kano, the Hong Kong crimelord. The other one was a big man in a cape.

"Hey, give me some of that," Kano said, grabbing some more food from a passing monk. Then Kano continued a story he had apparently been telling to the other man in the room.

"So then he freezes this guy and he shatters.

You can see his guts and everything! Almost lost my lunch!"

"Disgusting," said the man in the cape.

"And if that Shang Tsung guy's so great, how come he's got such a crummy looking boat?" Kano asked. "Guy gives me the creeps. 'Treasure these moments...'"

"Kano..." Sonya whispered, in her hiding-place on the ledge.

"That was his intention," said the man in the cape. "Shang Tsung is a great sorcerer. The wise cultivate his favor. Those who challenge his power... become his slaves."

"Haven't seen any slaves around," Kano said. He belched, covering his mouth with his hand, then reached for another plate of food.

"Shang Tsung enslaves souls," explained the man in the cape. "He learned the black arts from the emperor himself."

"Ah, yes, the emperor. You're some kinda royalty, too," Kano said.

"That's very perceptive of you," the man replied. "I am Goro, general of the armies of Outworld and Prince of the subterranean realm of Shokan." Goro stood and removed his cloak. He stretched his hands. He had strong shoulders— and four muscular arms.

THREE

"SUBTERRANEAN?" KANO asked. "That's something like...underground?"

"Yes, something like that," Goro replied.

"Yeah, well I'm kind of an underworld chief myself," Kano said. "You know, back home."

"How lucky for them...back home," Goro said.

As he spoke, Shang Tsung and his ninjas entered the throne room.

"It's true, Prince Goro," Shang said. "Why else would I choose such a disreputable-looking cretin? Look at him. No dignity. No manners. But in the realm of Earth, men like him can amass wealth and almost godlike power."

"Yeah, well, I'd like to get back to my amassing as soon as possible," Kano said. "When do I get paid?"

"After you've fought the girl," Shang told him. "That was our 'deal.' Only remember, she mustn't be harmed ... only humiliated. I have ... plans ... for the beautiful Sonya."

"Well, let me at her, then," Kano said. "Think I like hiding down here in a cave like some kinda slimy toad?"

Goro leaned forward until his huge head was level with Kano's. The Shokan prince leaned his hands on the table and stared at Kano.

"No offense intended," Kano said nervously.

"None taken," Goro said. He reached out one of his lower hands and lightly slapped Kano on the cheek. Then the four-armed giant stood and spoke directly to the demon sorcerer.

"To what do we owe the honor of your visit, Shang Tsung?" Goro said.

"I came to warn you that Kung Lao's descendant is competing in the tournament. You must handle him carefully."

"I saw this Liu Kang in the hall. He reminds me of his ancestor," Goro said. "He'll pose no problem."

"Don't underestimate the power and resourcefulness of these...humans! It will be your downfall," Shang said.

Goro looked at Shang in silence for a moment. Then he spoke aloud.

"You lost to Kung Lao, a common monk! I defeated him...and every human since...for the last five hundred years. This time will be no different."

"This is no time for foolish pride," Shang said angrily. "We have never been so close to absolute victory. Which is why I've come to tell you of another danger...the Princess Kitana."

"The Emperor's adopted daughter?" Goro asked. "Why should I worry about her?"

"Kitana is ten thousand years old and the rightful heir to the throne of Outworld," Shang explained. "She uses her age and wisdom to lead the rebellion against the emperor. She alone keeps alive the memory of the ancient realm before our benevolent master came and conquered. Her pathetic followers pose no threat to us in Outworld now...but she must not be allowed to join with the forces from the Realm of Earth. Especially Liu Kang!"

Johnny, Sonya, and Liu were still hidden on the ledge, listening carefully to what was being said below them.

"What's so special about you?" Johnny asked.

"I don't know," Liu replied in a whisper.

"The Emperor will not tolerate failure," Shang said, "and neither will I."

"I do not fail," Goro said.

Just then a jaguar roared. It was looking up at the ledge where Johnny and the others were hidden. Goro turned to look in that direction as well.

"Let's get out of here," Liu said to his two companions, speaking softly.

Kano noticed that Shang Tsung and Goro were no longer talking.

"What is it?" Kano asked.

"We aren't alone," Shang said.

Goro gestured to the Outworld guards who waited in the room, and pointed to the ledge. Johnny and his companions ran into a tunnel which led away from the cavern. Four of the guards started to chase them.

The tunnels were narrow and twisty. Eventually, the tunnel through which Johnny, Liu, and Sonya were running connected with several more tunnels to form a larger room.

The Outworld guards were still chasing the humans. All three of the fighters from the Realm of Earth could hear them. Liu pointed down the tunnel which joined theirs to the left. A woman dressed in red silk stood a distance away in that direction, holding a torch and gesturing to Liu to follow her.

"She must be the Princess Kitana," Liu said. "I think she's trying to help us."

"I think you're a little hard up for a date," Johnny said.

"Come on," said Liu. "She's trying to lead us out."

"Forget about her," Johnny said. "She's ten thousand years old!"

"Never underestimate the attraction of an older woman," Liu said.

"Are you nuts?" Johnny said. "Liu! I hate this!"

Liu didn't answer. He ran down the tunnel the princess had been standing in.

"Okay, so which way do we go?" Johnny asked Sonya.

"If this were one of your films," Sonya said, "you'd know the way out."

"So... you have seen my films. Which ones?" Johnny said.

"Does it matter?" Sonya asked. "They're all the same."

"They are not!" Johnny exclaimed.

"Yes they are!" Sonya insisted.

"They are not!"

"The woman is always in jeopardy, and you

always rescue her."

"Look, I don't want to talk about this anymore."

They followed in the direction Liu had gone.

Just then, in the room which Liu had entered, the reptilian creature Shang Tsung had spoken to earlier emerged from its hiding place. It had been invisible against the stone wall. It stepped in front of Liu and sprayed a stream of poison in his face. Liu dropped to the floor of the room, screaming.

"What happened, Liu?" Johnny asked a moment later when he arrived with Sonya.

"There's something... I think it's following Princess Kitana," Liu said.

"Which way did Kitana go?" Sonya asked.

"I don't know," Liu replied.

"Great!" Sonya said.

"All right," Johnny said. "This way. Well, come on, then...."

Liu asked, "Do you know where you're going?"

"Relax, I know exactly where we're going. Princess Kitana went this way. I can smell her perfume," Johnny said.

They came out of the tunnel, in the cavern where they had started. Goro and Kano were gone, but six Outworld guards remained, armed with lances.

"Okay. Six of them," Johnny said, glancing around the room. "Not to worry. That's two each."

"You can count," Sonya said. "I sure hope you can fight."

The guards split up. Sonya was left facing one, Liu was facing two, and Johnny saw the remaining three walking toward him, holding their lances in front of them.

"Three? How come I get three?" Johnny asked.

Then the fighting began. The Outworld guards were good fighters, strong and fast, but the three humans were stronger and faster. They soon beat the guards.

"Just the way I like them," Sonya said, looking at the six guards lying on the ground. "Dumb and ugly."

"Piece of cake," Johnny said.

"Piece of cake, huh?" Liu said.

"Well, it was easy for me," Johnny said.

"Oh, get over yourself!" Sonya said.

"What is it with you guys?" Johnny said. "We're standing, they're not! What more do you want?"

All at once the three were aware of someone else in the room—an old man dressed like a peasant. The newcomer was Rayden.

"Congratulations!" Rayden said. "Now show me what you plan to do about . . . them!"

Hundreds more Outworld guards were silently filling the cavern.

FOUR

✦✦✦

Sonya, Liu, and Johnny took defensive stances. But before a fight could break out, Rayden stood and walked between the humans and the outworlders.

"I don't think so," Rayden said. "Wait for Mortal Kombat to begin." The god of lightning turned to the three humans.

"This," he said, "is the way out."

"Catch you later, guys," Johnny said to the guards, giving a cheerful wave with his hand.

"Now you've seen what you'll be facing in the tournament," Rayden said, when all four of them reached the garden again.

"You mean Goro?" Johnny asked.

"And Shang Tsung," Rayden said.

"Will Shang Tsung fight in the tournament?" Liu asked.

"If he chooses," Rayden said. "As a former champion he has that right. And he's far more dangerous than Goro. His demon power comes from the souls of vanquished warriors.... To fight Shang Tsung is to face not one, but a legion of adversaries. Remember that."

"Then how can we win?" Sonya asked.

"Goro can be killed," Rayden replied. "Shang Tsung's power can be destroyed by mortal men and women. You can overcome any adversary, no matter how bizarre their powers may seem. There is always a way! Only one thing can defeat you...your own fear."

"Who says we're afraid?" Johnny asked.

"You must first face your fears if you are to conquer them," Rayden said. "You, Johnny, are afraid you're a fake. So, you'll rush into any fight to prove you're not. You'll fight...bravely enough...but foolishly...carelessly...and you'll be beaten. You, Sonya, are afraid to admit even you sometimes need help. If you are afraid to trust...you will lose."

"What about me?" Liu asked.

"You fear your own destiny," Rayden replied. "You already fled it once, when you went to America ... and now that fear has brought you guilt for the death of your brother."

"I am responsible for Chan's death," Liu said.

"No!" Rayden exclaimed. "Every mortal is responsible for his own destiny. Chan believed this. Why can't you?"

"I've tried!"

"Despair is the most dangerous fear of all," Rayden said. "Guilt over the past ... dread of the future. These are your enemies. I know all this. And so does Shang Tsung."

"How?" Liu asked.

"He can peer into your soul and use the fear he sees there against you," Rayden replied. "Tomorrow the tournament begins. You must be prepared!

Dawn rose over the island. Shang Tsung sat on a throne overlooking the tournament grounds. Many black-hooded monks stood around him. Silence fell as Shang rose to speak.

"From this moment on," Shang Tsung cried, "my island will be your battleground. Let Mortal Kombat begin!"

Monks holding scrolls walked among the fighters, taking them to the arenas where their bouts were to take place.

Liu was surprised when he saw his opponent. It was Princess Kitana. He felt unsure of himself. He had thought that the princess was his friend, yet here she was, fighting against him.

She attacked, and he blocked, but did not counterattack.

The princess's eyes grew cold. She tripped him, knocking him to the ground, then pinned him. Her lips were close to his ear.

She whispered in his ear: "To win your next match, use the element that brings life."

"What?" Liu asked, puzzled. He broke free. When he looked outside the ring, he saw Shang Tsung watching.

Ah, Liu thought. That's it! This is how Kitana has arranged to speak to me without Shang suspecting. If I don't win this bout, her message will do me no good.

With a dazzling display of skill, Liu attacked the princess. No matter what Kitana did, she couldn't stop him. Liu pinned her to the mat.

"Remember my words," Kitana said. Then the monk approached to give the bout to Liu, and mark the victory on his scroll.

26

*   *   *

A hooded monk led Johnny Cage to a fighting ring. The monk bowed and moved aside, and Johnny could see his opponent. It was Scorpion, one of Shang's ninjas.

Scorpion thrust his hand forward. A spikelike creature flew from his palm, straight toward Johnny. The spike was attached to a long cord, leading back to the ninja.

At the last moment, Johnny ducked under the spike. The spike buried itself in the ground.

"Missed me," Johnny said. He pulled out a knife and slashed the cord connecting the spike to Scorpion. The ninja howled in rage.

Scorpion raised his other hand to shoot another spike.

"Hey, I've already seen your rope trick," Johnny said. "Show me something new."

He ran toward Scorpion. When he got close enough, he leapt into the air, delivering his famous shadow kick. The ninja fell unconscious.

"Like that," Johnny said. He pulled out a pair of dark glasses and slipped them on.

The monk marked down the victory on his scroll.

A monk led Liu into the Great Hall.

"My match is here?" Liu asked.

In answer the monk bowed and stepped back. Liu turned to look around the hall. A figure was standing at the top of the stairs. It was Sub-Zero, another one of Shang's ninjas.

The ninja approached. Liu took his stance. Then the fight began. It ranged up and down the length of the Great Hall. Liu used all of his skill and strength. He was faster than the ninja. Just a little faster. The battle was going his way.

A sudden blast of cold struck Liu. He saw a blue glow surround Sub-Zero.

"Oh, no," Liu said. He knew how fast the cold could get to him. There wasn't time for him to reach Sub-Zero from where he was standing to defend himself. Liu took a step back, kicking over a bucket of water. The water froze as it spilled across the floor. Kitana's words came to him.

"Use the force that brings life," Liu whispered. "Water!"

Liu picked up a second pail of water, still attached to a carrying handle. He swung it around and around his head, faster and faster. He let it go, and the bucket of water flew toward Sub-Zero.

As the bucket tumbled through the air, it

spilled water. The ninja let loose his cold blast. The blast struck the water, freezing it into a long spear of ice.

Before Sub-Zero could move out of the way, the icicle hit him, pinning him to a pillar. Sub-Zero looked down in disbelief as his own weapon was turned against him. Slowly, from the center out, the ninja froze into a glittering sculpture of solid ice.

Liu looked up from the sight of the frozen ninja. Princess Kitana was watching from a distance.

The monk marked down the victory on his scroll.

Prince Goro of Shokan, the reigning champion, sat brooding on his throne. He looked up as a figure entered the underground room. Shang Tsung stood before him.

"Is it time?" Goro asked.

"Yes," Shang replied. "We've let these humans win enough."

"At last," Goro said. He rose, stretching himself to his full height. Then he fastened his cape around his shoulders and walked from the room.

The sun was setting over the island. Drums beat in the Great Hall. A group of Outworld warriors, impressive in their bone armor, cleared a space in the center of the room.

"Now for the final bout of the day," Shang said. "The fighter from the Realm of Earth who has won the most bouts will have the honor of fighting the champion of Outworld."

Goro strode into the hall behind the warriors.

A monk was leading in a man, a human fighter. It was Art Lean, a martial arts champion.

At the other side of the ring of warriors, Goro had removed his cape. Art Lean advanced to the center of the ring and bowed to the four-armed giant.

Goro returned the bow with equal formality. Then both fighters took their defensive stances. A moment passed before either moved. Then Art attacked, punching and kicking. Goro didn't seem to feel the blows.

Art leapt into the air, delivering a staggering kick that knocked Goro half a step backward. The Prince of Shokan bellowed with rage, then counterattacked.

Art dodged the fists of his opponent, but he couldn't get through the four-armed defense to follow up his earlier victory.

Then Goro reached out with his two lower

arms and grabbed the human fighter. The crowd fell silent.

"You fought well," Goro said.

"Finish him!" Shang called.

FIVE

❖❖❖

THE SHOKAN giant looked at Shang, then began to pummel Art Lean with his two free hands. Art slumped in his grasp.

"Bring him to me," Shang said. "His soul is mine."

Goro carried Art's body to Shang. The emperor's sorcerer reached out his hand and pulled Art's soul from his body, making the spirit into another of his captive warriors.

The shrieking of a thousand other imprisoned souls filled the hall.

"Excellent," Shang said. "Flawless victory."

A monk marked the victory on his scroll.

*   *   *

Johnny, Liu, and Sonya turned away in shock and horror. They saw Rayden standing before them, dressed as a coolie.

"You could have stopped that," Liu said.

"I told you," Rayden replied sadly. "I cannot interfere."

"That's why I left the temple!" Liu said, anger burning within him. "All this mumbo jumbo about the power of reason and light. Where are you when we need you? Where is that power?"

"The power is in you," Rayden said. "If the gods decide men's destiny, then there is no free will. No choice. In Outworld, the emperor makes every decision. You have only to obey. Is that what you want?"

"What choice did he have?" Liu asked, pointing to where Art Lean lay silent and still on the floor of the Great Hall.

"He chose to fight and die a free man," Rayden said. "If Outworld wins this tournament, no mortal man will ever have that choice again!"

"How can I defeat a sorcerer like Shang Tsung? I'm not my ancestor. You were right. I'm not ready!"

"The true warrior learns from his own experience," Rayden said. "You have carved your own path to this place and this moment! Everything you need is within you now, Liu Kang. Unlock that power and you will win."

Lord Rayden turned, and in a moment had vanished again in the crowd of humans and Outworlders.

Next morning the sun rose out of the deep blue ocean. On top of the cliff overlooking the sea far below, Johnny Cage was practicing his moves, using a chain as his weapon. Sonya Blade approached, watching a moment to see him work out. The chain was whipping in complex patterns, nearly too fast to see.

"Johnny?" Sonya said at last.

Johnny finished his routine and turned to face her.

"Go ahead, say it," Johnny said. "You're impressed."

He waited a moment for a reaction. "Aha! Is that a smile?"

"What are you doing?" Sonya asked, ignoring his last remark.

"I always charge into things without thinking," Johnny said. "So this time I'm working on a strategy."

"A strategy?" Sonya echoed.

"If we don't have a strategy, Goro will kill us

off, one by one," Johnny explained, looping the chain in his hand.

"You're going to stop Goro, all by yourself? You're going to protect us from the big bad monster, is that it? Just like in your movies?"

"I'm going to challenge Goro. Shang Tsung won't be expecting that. I figure he—"

"You can't do that!" Sonya said. "It's not how the tournament works."

"I can beat him!" Johnny said.

"You can beat him!" Sonya exploded. "*You* can beat him! You are the most egotistical, self-deluded, stupid person I've ever met!"

"What? Because I don't want to see anyone else bludgeoned to death for Shang Tsung's entertainment?"

"Don't you dare do this to protect me, Johnny Cage!"

"You!" Johnny exploded. "You think I'm talking about you! You call me egotistical?" He paused. "Wait a minute. Are you worried about me?"

"Ooh! Listen to him! You're being absurd."

"You are worried."

"I am not."

"You are. You like me," Johnny said.

"You wish!" Sonya said. She turned and walked off, not looking back.

Johnny watched her go. "The girl's in love," he said. Then he returned to his workout and practice, while the sun rose, and a gentle breeze blew over the gardens.

Sonya found Liu Kang on the tournament field overlooking the arenas where the fighting was already taking place.

"How are we doing?" she asked.

"We're getting destroyed," Liu replied.

A group of black-cowled monks walked past, carrying a human fighter in their arms. The man was unconscious, his arms hanging limp.

"That good, eh?" Sonya said with grim humor.

A voice from behind startled them. Liu and Sonya turned, to find Shang Tsung standing amid a group of monks.

"I have a present for you," Shang said, looking directly at Sonya.

"I don't want anything from you," Sonya told him.

"That's not true," Shang said. "There is one thing you want very much."

Shang turned, and looked behind him. Sonya followed his glance. Kano, the crime lord, was waiting there inside the ring. He was stripped to the waist, ready for battle. His red eye was glowing.

Shang stepped aside. A monk holding a scroll walked up to Sonya and led her to the ring.

"Sonya—stay cool," Liu said.

Sonya stepped into the ring and waited for Kano. She looked at him with a frozen expression.

"How ya doin', babe?" Kano said, his features twisting in a smile. "Did you miss me?"

"Not particularly," Sonya said. "I'm here to bring you back to justice."

"Justice? Some other time," Kano said. He reached into his boot and pulled out a knife. It flashed as he tossed it from hand to hand and spun it in his fingers.

"This baby brings back memories," he said.

"You used it to stab your mother in the back?" Sonya asked.

"Guess again," Kano said. "It put a big smile on your partner—from ear to ear."

Sonya moved into a fighting crouch, hands before her. She attacked. Kano blocked easily. Then it was Kano's turn to attack, and it was all Sonya could do to keep the whirling knife from cutting her.

"It won't help you," Kano said. "I've studied all your moves, sweetheart."

Sonya's face grew pale. She jumped into a handstand, then dropped her legs around Kano's

37

neck. The knife flew from his hand as they fell to the ground.

"Study *this*!" Sonya snarled. She squeezed Kano's neck. His face grew red, and he clawed at her legs, but there was nothing he could do to break the grip.

Shang Tsung leaned closer. He watched Kano's face with deep interest.

"Don't do it, Sonya—that's what he wants!" Liu called.

"That's right. Finish him!" Shang shouted. "Pay me tribute with his death!"

The sound of shrieking souls, the slaves of Shang Tsung, echoed over the field. The same sound had filled the Great Hall the night before, when Shang took Art Lean's spirit. Kano had gone limp.

"If you kill him, Sonya, Shang Tsung will own you," Liu said quietly.

"No!" Sonya shouted. She let go of her grip on Kano's neck and stood away from the unconscious thug.

"You disappoint me," Shang said. "That isn't wise."

"I don't answer to you," Sonya replied.

"One day soon," Shang said, "you will. All of you will!"

The sorcerer turned and stalked away, sur-rounded by his servants.

Silently a monk recorded Sonya's victory on his scroll.

"Goro! Goro!" Johnny shouted.

The actor was standing in the statuary garden, shouting the name of the Shokan prince. Johnny was wearing his fighting costume.

"Goro! Goro!"

Shang Tsung approached Johnny, stopping at a slight distance. The warriors and monks who accompanied the emperor's sorcerer stopped as well.

"Is there something you want?" Shang asked.

"A Big Mac and a large order of fries," Johnny replied casually, "but I'll settle for that tub of lard with the four arms."

"You're challenging Goro?" Shang asked, amused. "You weren't supposed to fight him now. Are you that eager to die?"

SIX

✦✦✦

SHANG PAUSED. Johnny looked at him.

"I'm not the one who's going to die," Johnny said.

"I see," Shang said. He looked into Johnny's eyes. "You're very foolish. You think that you can protect your friends. Make no mistake. They, too, will die—after Goro has destroyed you."

"Then what's the problem?" Johnny asked. "Get this Goro guy out here."

"As absurd as your demand is, I will grant it," Shang said. "In return, I reserve the right to challenge the winner—or another of my choosing

—at the place appointed by me for the final battle of the tournament."

"You got it, pal!" Johnny said.

While Johnny and Shang were talking, an old man dressed in a beggar's rags approached. When he looked up, everybody knew at once by his glowing eyes that the beggar was really Lord Rayden.

"No!" Rayden shouted. "This match should not take place!"

"The rules are quite clear, Lord Rayden," Shang said. "How do you say it? 'A deal's a deal'?"

Shang walked off, laughing.

Rayden stood in the garden, under the shadows of the statues, facing Johnny.

"What have you done?" Rayden demanded.

"Exercised my own free will," Johnny said, glaring at Rayden. His breath was coming quickly. "Made a choice. This is our tournament, remember? Mortal Kombat! We humans fight it!"

Rayden waited a moment for Johnny to calm himself. Finally the god of lightning spoke.

"Good," Rayden said. "At last, one of you has understood."

Liu Kang and Sonya had approached while Rayden was talking with Johnny. They, too, looked at the movie actor with appraising eyes.

The Outworlders had swept the garden near the mouth of the tunnel to Goro's domain. Drums beat wildly. Fighters from all over the island were gathering outside the line of Outworld warriors.

Liu stood in the crowd with Sonya beside him. Another fighter walked past—Princess Kitana, with her four-ladies-in waiting beside her.

"Liu Kang, your turn will come," Kitana said.

"How?" Liu asked. "Whoever wins, it's over."

"No," Kitana replied. "It's not over yet."

"What do you mean?" Liu asked.

"Trust me," Kitana replied.

Johnny stood in the empty space cleared by the warriors. He leaned against a statue, wearing his dark glasses. The length of chain he'd practiced with earlier hung casually from his right hand.

The drums beat louder. Goro appeared from the tunnel, his silk cape streaming out behind him. He raised all four arms to the sky and cried out a warrior's challenge. The sound echoed over the island.

"You're gonna hurt yourself yelling like that," Johnny said.

The Shokan prince paused for a moment, tilted his head, and looked at Johnny.

"Strange," Goro said. "We've barely met, and

already I don't like you."

"Impossible," Johnny said. "Everybody likes me."

"I'm going to enjoy dismembering you," Goro said.

The monks who stood near the two fighters moved quickly away.

"Let's dance," Johnny said.

Goro snapped out a punch. Johnny flipped his chain against Goro's knuckles, then did several backflips to get away from the four-armed giant's attack. He disappeared behind a statue in the garden.

"What's he doing?" Liu asked.

"He said he was working on a strategy," Sonya said.

"This is a strategy?" Liu asked, puzzled.

Goro walked cautiously toward the statue where Johnny had vanished. All at once, the chain whipped out from behind a different statue, wrapping around one of Goro's four wrists, breaking it.

"So the little puppy has a bite," Goro said. The Shokan warrior dived toward Johnny, but Johnny leapt away, wrapping his chain around Goro's ankle as he did so. Another yank, and the ankle broke as well. Goro reached down, fast as lightning, and grabbed the chain. He pulled it from Johnny's grasp and flung it away. Goro rose to his feet and limped painfully after his now-disarmed opponent.

"Get away from him!" Liu called. "Remember what happened to Art!"

Johnny was boxed in by statues. Goro's fist smashed into Johnny's ribs, knocking him into a pedestal and driving the wind out of him. Johnny took another punch to the body, then a kick that sent him flying. He lay motionless on the ground.

"Johnny! Get up!" Liu yelled.

The loud howling of the lost souls trapped inside Shang began to rise.

"Johnny! Johnny, please!" Sonya cried.

"Where is my tribute?" Shang asked.

Goro knelt and scooped up Johnny's body in his two lower arms. He turned and slowly limped toward Shang. He stood for a moment before the demon sorcerer, then went on one knee to offer Johnny to him. As Goro raised Johnny's still form up toward Shang, Johnny came suddenly to life and, with a terrific cry, landed a karate punch between Goro's eyes.

"Aiyaah!" Johnny yelled.

Goro dropped Johnny and staggered back in pain and amazement. Johnny grabbed the four-armed giant's ponytail and looped it around the creature's neck. Then he braced himself against Goro's shoulders and, using his strength and leverage, pulled back hard. The prince began to strangle. He gasped, unable to breathe or speak.

"What's the matter?" Johnny said. "Having a bad hair day?"

Goro threw himself backward, trying to crush Johnny, but Johnny let go. He smashed Goro with his foot, causing the giant to roll over the edge of the cliff. Goro hung there with his one good upper hand. Far below, the clouds that surrounded the island twisted and churned, hiding the view of the beach a mile below. A stiff wind tousled Johnny's hair as he stood on the edge of the cliff, looking down.

"Finish him!" Shang said.

SEVEN

"No . . ." GORO said.

"So you can steal his soul?" Johnny asked. "I've won. That's enough."

"His soul now," Shang exclaimed, "or yours later!"

Johnny ignored the sorcerer. Instead he found the length of chain that he'd lost earlier. Bracing himself, he hung the end over the edge of the cliff, where Goro could take it with his lower hands.

"Go on. Grab hold," Johnny said.

"So I can crawl back to my cave and die in disgrace?" Goro asked. "I am a Shokan warrior! We die in battle!"

"You fought well," Johnny said.

Goro smiled up at Johnny. "As did you," he said.

With that he pushed away from the cliff and fell—down, down, down. Still falling, he vanished into the clouds below.

Johnny turned away.

A black-robed monk recorded the victory on his scroll.

"Well done," Rayden said.

"It's over," Johnny said. "The humans won and the Realm of Earth is safe. I defeated the champion!"

"It isn't over quite that quickly," Shang said. "Remember the promise you made? I reserved the right to challenge the winner—or another of my choosing—at a place appointed by me. That shall be the final battle of the tournament."

"Well, here I am," Johnny said. He swung his chain slowly from side to side. "Let's go."

"No," Shang said. "I choose *her!*"

With that, he grabbed Sonya Blade. Instantly the two of them were surrounded by a whirlwind of flying dust. It spread, growing larger, hiding them from view.

"You're a coward, Sorcerer!" Rayden said in a voice of thunder. "Stand and fight!"

"The rules of the tournament are quite clear, Lord Rayden," said Shang. "Mortal Kombat continues. I'm simply changing the place, as we agreed."

Shang and Sonya vanished.

"Sonya!" Johnny shouted. "Where has he taken her?"

"To the emperor's castle in the wastelands of Outworld, where I cannot follow," Rayden said.

"But I can," Liu said. "I'm going after them."

"Not without me, you're not," Johnny said. He turned to Lord Rayden. "Rayden—can Sonya beat Shang Tsung?"

"No," Rayden said, his voice grim. "I'm sorry. However, there is one last rule—although Shang Tsung neglected to mention it."

"I know what the rule is," Liu said. "It's in the legends. She has to accept the challenge, or there can be no final combat."

"You know Sonya," Johnny said. "She'll never back down. I've got to stop her! I can fight Shang Tsung!"

"Johnny Cage, you have played your part splendidly, but this battle, you cannot win," Rayden said.

"Then who can?" Johnny asked.

In answer Rayden merely looked at Liu.

"Okay, I get it," Johnny said. "How do we get to Outworld?"

"We're already there," Liu said.

"I have nothing further to teach you, Liu Kang," Rayden said. "You possess the knowledge to defeat Shang Tsung. All that is lacking now is the will."

"Are you sure you don't want to come?" Johnny asked Rayden.

"In Outworld, if you look hard enough, you will have another guide," Rayden replied. "Good luck."

The whirlwind from Shang's disappearance spread. Thunderous storm clouds swept across the island. All light disappeared. A moment later the clouds broke apart to show Johnny that he and Liu were standing on a road in the remnants of an ancient city. A dark tower stood on a mountain spur, brooding over the city.

"So where are we, O Chosen One?" Johnny asked, looking around.

"Where we've always been: Outworld," Liu said. "The island was an illusion created by Shang Tsung to make us believe we were still on Earth. We crossed into Outworld that night on the ship."

"So this is Outworld? I can see why they would

want a change of scenery," Johnny said. The land was dreary and bleak, covered with ash and soot. The sky was dark and smoky.

"We should head for that tower," Liu said, pointing. "Shang Tsung will have taken Sonya there."

"Scary-looking place."

"The legends say the emperor built it on the burial mound of his enemies."

"Guy had a lot of enemies," Johnny said. The two fighters started walking.

In the Black Tower, Sonya stood facing Shang in the center of a courtyard decorated with the Mortal Kombat symbol, surrounded by dozens of torches.

"Why have you brought me here?" Sonya demanded. "Why not Liu or Johnny? Are you afraid of them?"

"I fear no human," Shang said. "I brought you here to be my queen. I can lay the Realm of Earth at your feet, Sonya, and fulfill your every fantasy. I can see into your soul. You'd like to let your defenses down and give yourself to a man who is your equal. I am that man. I will defeat you in the final battle, and then I will spare you. We will live happily ever after."

"What if I refuse to fight?"

"You? Back down from a challenge?" Shang said, incredulously. "When have you ever done that? It's simply not in your nature."

"Human beings can change. Besides, Johnny Cage will come after me."

"I hope he does," Shang said. "You can watch me destroy him."

"He beat Goro."

"He can't beat me. If you want to spare him, you will fight me. Then I will enter the Realm of Earth triumphantly with my benevolent master. And you, Sonya, will be at my side."

On the road outside the castle, a hooded figure met Johnny and Liu.

"Kitana!" Liu said.

"Come with me," Kitana said. "We must hurry."

"What happened here?" Liu asked, gesturing around him to indicate the city.

"The same thing that will happen to your entire world, unless you prevent it. My father was the rightful ruler of Outworld. Then his best warriors lost ten Mortal Kombats, and the emperor entered the realm, killed my parents, and adopted me to lay claim to the throne. This place was beautiful once, before Shang Tsung engineered its destruction."

The three walked toward the Black Tower. Beneath its gates they met a group of robed and hooded monks walking in. Johnny, Liu, and Kitana joined the end of the procession.

"How can I possibly stop this from happening to my world?" Liu asked.

"You must win, Liu Kang," Kitana said. "In the Black Tower you will face three challenges. You must face your enemy, you must face yourself, and you must face your worst fear."

EIGHT

✦❖✦

MEANWHILE, IN the courtyard—"I won't fight you, Shang Tsung!" Sonya snapped. "I'm not playing into your game, whatever it is."

"There is no one else from Earth here to accept the challenge. If you don't fight, the Realm of Earth will forfeit the tournament, and its portals will open to our great emperor."

"You're bluffing. My friends are coming!"

"Hoping against hope is such an endearing human trait," Shang said. "I'm touched. Really. This is your last chance. Fight me in Mortal Kombat."

"No!"

Shang looked at the monks. "Take her away. The emperor will be overjoyed."

Three monks stepped forward, cowls hiding their faces.

"My friends will come," Sonya said.

One of the monks who had stepped forward threw off his hood, revealing Johnny Cage.

"Her friends are here already," Johnny said.

"Right on cue," Shang said. "So much like an actor. Are you challenging me now?"

"No," Liu said, also throwing off his hood. "I am."

"Seize them!" Shang cried.

"Stay where you are," said the third monk, removing her hood to reveal Princess Kitana. "Would you dare interfere with the tournament?" she asked. "Mortal Kombat cannot be won by treachery! That is the law!"

Johnny, Sonya, and Kitana turned to Liu, watching him expectantly.

"I am the Chosen One, descendant of Kung Lao!" Liu said. "I challenge you to Mortal Kombat! Do you accept or yield?"

For a long moment the four stood facing the sorcerer as he looked from face to face.

At last Shang said, "I accept."

The monks backed away. Johnny, Kitana, and Sonya went with them. The edge of the arena lowered to reveal a pit filled with spikes surrounding the fighting area. A weird howling arose from the center of the arena.

"What is that sound?" Johnny shouted.

"The source of all Shang Tsung's power," Kitana said. "The souls of a thousand dead warriors crying out."

Liu approached Shang. The sorcerer backed away.

"You can't run from me," Liu said.

"You fool," Shang said. "I have within me an army of slave souls to fight you. I don't need to run." Suddenly six ghostly warriors appeared and surrounded Liu.

Liu did not hesitate. With an awesome display of fighting skill, he defeated them, one after another. They evaporated as they touched the ground. At last Liu stood alone in the ring facing Shang Tsung.

"Send your slave warriors, Sorcerer!" Liu shouted. "Send them all! Your conjurer's tricks have no power over me."

"Liu Kang," Shang said, "I can see into your soul. You will die."

"You can look into my soul," Liu said, "but you

don't own it. I'm not afraid of my destiny."

"You have faced yourself," Kitana said. "Now face your worst fear."

Suddenly Shang changed. His features became those of Chan, Liu's brother.

"No," Liu shouted. "It's not really you."

"Rayden sent me," Chan said. "To help you."

"You're not Chan," Liu whispered.

"Remember when our parents left?" Chan said. "You promised to always take care of me. Now it is my turn to take care of you. I forgive you for letting me die."

"No," Liu said. "It wasn't me who killed you. Shang Tsung killed my brother!"

Liu concentrated on the form before him. Suddenly he could see through Chan, and see Shang Tsung behind him.

"Face your enemy," Kitana said.

The ghostly chorus of howling voices increased in volume.

"You hear them, Sorcerer," Liu said. "You hear your slaves. You're losing your power over them. They have risen against you! You can't command them now! Free them!"

"No! They are mine, forever," Shang said.

"All those souls and you still don't have one of your own. I pity you, Sorcerer."

"Pity is for the weak!"

"Your slave demons have failed you. Your dark magic is worthless. You've lost, Sorcerer!"

"No!" Shang shouted.

Liu ran and leapt. His foot flashed out, taking Shang in the chest. The demon sorcerer fell into the pit filled with spikes. The humans had won, and a monk wrote down the victory on his scroll.

"Flawless victory," Liu said. "The Realm of Earth is safe."